C L A S S I C
ANIMAL
TALES

READER'S DIGEST YOUNG FAMILIES, INC.

Cover illustrated by Richard Bernal

Title page illustrated by Jason Wolff

This edition is published by Reader's Digest Young Families, Inc.

Pleasantville, NY 10570

www.readersdigest.com

Reader's Digest Young Families is a trademark of The Reader's Digest Association, Inc.

Louis Weber, C.E.O.

Publications International, Ltd.

7373 North Cicero Avenue

Lincolnwood, Illinois 60712

www.pubint.com

Manufactured in China.

8 7 6 5 4 3 2 1

ISBN: 0-7853-4739-9

CONTENTS

The City Mouse and the Country Mouse

Once upon a time a country mouse named Oliver lived in a hole under the root of a big old oak tree. Oliver loved the sound of squirrels chattering during the day and crickets chirping at night. He loved the smell of rich dirt and hearty grass all around him.

One day Oliver invited his city cousin, Alistair, for a visit. Before Alistair arrived, Oliver tidied up his hole. He straightened his oak leaf bed. He spread fresh pine needles on the floor. He scrubbed the tuna can he used for a table and polished the bottle caps he used as plates.

Then Oliver sat by the entrance to his hole, gazed out at the stars, and waited for his cousin Alistair to arrive.

When Alistair arrived, he set his fine leather suitcase on the rug of pine needles. "I say, cousin, is this your cellar?" he asked Oliver.

"No," said Oliver, "it's my home."

Oliver showed Alistair the back of the hole and the storeroom where he stored all of his grain. He led Alistair up onto the knob of the old oak root, where he sometimes sat to watch the sunset. Then he sat Alistair down at the tuna can table and served him a fabulous dinner of barleycorn and wheat germ.

Alistair nibbled his meal politely. "This certainly tastes as though it's good for me." He coughed and swallowed. "A bit dry, perhaps. Could I bother you for a cup of tea?"

Oliver brewed up a thimble of dandelion tea. When the thimble was empty, Oliver changed into his long johns, Alistair changed into his silk pajamas, and the mice settled into their oak leaves for the night.

Oliver awoke early the next morning, as usual. A robin family twittered in the old oak tree. A rooster crowed at a nearby farm.

Alistair squeezed his pillow over his ears. "What is that confounded racket?" he mumbled.

"That's the sound of morning in the country," said Oliver. "It's the wonderful music that makes me want to leap from my bed each morning and start the new day."

Alistair pulled the pillow from his face and opened one eye. "You start your day in the morning?" he asked. "Good heavens, cousin, I usually don't rise till noon."

"Here in the country we rise at dawn," Oliver replied as he buttoned his overalls. Then he pulled on his work boots and pushed his wheelbarrow out into the morning sun.

Alistair rolled to the edge of his oak leaf bed. He slid his feet into his shiny black dress shoes and followed his cousin outside.

Oliver gathered acorns and stacked them near his hole.

Alistair yawned and leaned against the root of the old oak tree.

Oliver shucked the seeds from the tall rye grass and carried them to the back of his hole where they would stay dry.

Alistair wiped the dust from his shoes with his silk handkerchief.

Oliver ventured into a nearby field to find fallen cornstalks. He dragged several of the stalks home and peeled off the husks. Oliver then rubbed the kernels of corn loose and one by one piled them neatly against the root of the old oak.

"There." Oliver rubbed his hands on his overalls. "That's done."

"Thank goodness." Alistair collapsed into the wheelbarrow. "Now that we've finished the work, I'd say it's time for a bit of a snack and a nap. Wouldn't you?"

Oliver giggled. "The work isn't finished. We still have to carry in water and hack out that root that is growing down into my kitchen. And winter is coming, don't forget. Time to gather up rags and bits of grass to keep the hole snug and warm."

Alistair sighed. "I'm simply not cut out for the country life," he said. "You work too hard for your dinner. And all you end up with is a pile of birdseed. A mouse could starve to death here. Come home with me for a while. I'll show you the good life."

Alistair packed his silk pajamas into his fine leather suitcase. Oliver packed his long johns into his beat-up carpet bag. The two mice set out for Alistair's home in the city.

Oliver followed Alistair over fields and valleys, into subway tunnels, and through crowded city streets until they reached the luxury hotel where Alistair lived.

Alistair stopped in front of the door. "Polished marble floors and shiny brass knobs," he said. "This is how mice are supposed to live."

Oliver stared up at the revolving glass door. "H-h-how do we get inside, Alistair?"

"Wait till the opening comes around, then run through as fast as you can," Alistair replied. The door swung around, and Alistair quickly disappeared inside.

CITY

Oliver took a deep breath. He saw an opening and dove inside. He tried to run through, like Alistair had said, but his carpet bag was caught on the edge of the door. Oliver went round and round. He spun so many times, he couldn't tell whether he was right side up, or upside-down.

Oliver whirled and whirled, and might still be whirling to this very day if Alistair hadn't leaped up, tugged the bag free, and dragged his dizzy friend inside.

Oliver sat on the marble floor to catch his breath. Then he followed Alistair across the lobby and through a small crack in the wall hidden by velvet draperies.

"My apartment," Alistair said when they were inside.

Oliver looked around in amazement. Alistair's home was filled with gold candlesticks, crystal goblets, and linen napkins embroidered with the hotel's name.

"We're under the bandstand." Alistair pointed out the hole that was his front door. "An orchestra plays, and ladies and gentlemen dance every night until dawn."

"How can you sleep with all the noise?" asked Oliver.

"Sleep?" said Alistair. "I can sleep during the day. We do things a little differently here. Dinner, for example. At a five-star hotel, dinner begins with hors d'oeuvres."

Alistair led Oliver through the dining room. They hid behind potted plants and raced under tablecloths. They waited until the chef went to check something in the dining room, then scampered across the kitchen and into the pantry.

The pantry was dark. Oliver stumbled. Something skidded across the pantry and thwack!

"Do be careful," said Alistair. He opened the pantry door a crack.

In the dim light Oliver could barely see what he'd stumbled over. "It's a-a-a . . . oh my!"

"A mousetrap." Alistair scooted it under a shelf with his paw. "You'll learn to stay away from them."

Alistair led Oliver up the shelves to the hors d'oeuvres. Alistair gobbled fancy crackers, nibbled pasta, and even managed to chew a hole in a tin of smoked salmon.

"Now this," said Alistair, patting his tummy, "is fine dining."

Oliver was still so frightened, that he barely ate a crumb.

"Tonight the chef is preparing roast duckling with herbed potatoes in a delicate cream sauce." Alistair's mouth watered. His whiskers twitched. "One taste and you'll never go back to the country."

The mice crept out of the pantry. The kitchen was empty. They scurried under the chef's work table.

"Our chef is quite a messy fellow," said Alistair. "He drops chunks of meat and potatoes and dollops of sauce all over the floor. One evening I found an entire turkey drumstick lying under the stove."

Alistair darted about, gathering up bits of duckling and potatoes. He didn't notice the chef marching back into the kitchen.

But the chef noticed Alistair.

"You again!" shouted the chef. "And this time you've brought a friend. Furry little pests! I will not have you in my five-star kitchen." The chef grabbed a broom and chased the mice round and round the kitchen.

Alistair and Oliver escaped through a hole under the sink.

"No main course tonight, I'm afraid," said Alistair. "But don't worry, cousin. We'll make up for it with dessert."

Alistair led Oliver around the water pipes and through the walls. They squeezed through a gap in the baseboard, and Oliver still found himself in the enormous kitchen, but this time he was directly beneath the pastry cart. The chef thought the two mice had escaped him and he gave up his search.

Alistair showed Oliver the tarts and turnovers and cheesecakes. He demonstrated how to flick bits of meringue off a pie with his tail.

Oliver timidly nibbled the edge of a flaky cream puff. It was the most delicious thing he had ever tasted. He leaned forward to get a bigger bite and splat!

The cart lurched forward. Oliver landed face down in the cream puff. Alistair grabbed the edge of a lacy napkin and hung on tight as a waiter wheeled the cart across the dining room.

The cart clanked to a stop near Alistair's apartment. The waiter snatched up three plates of cherry cheesecake and bustled away.

Oliver wobbled off the cart and sank down in the plush carpet to catch his breath. "I'm not cut out for life in the city," he said. "You take too many risks for your dinner. A mouse could starve to death here, too. There is plenty of delicious food, but I'm too frightened to eat any of it. I'm going home to the good life."

So Oliver dragged his carpet bag back through crowded city streets, into subway tunnels, and over fields and valleys until he reached his hole under the root of the big old oak tree.

He ate a late supper of acorns and wheat kernels, then curled up in his oak leaf bed. He could hear the crickets chirping, and he could see the fireflies flickering.

Back at his hotel, Alistair licked meringue from his whiskers and curled up in his linen napkin. He listened to the orchestra and watched all the glistening gowns as couples twirled by on the dance floor.

Both mice sighed at the very same time. "I love being home," they said and slowly drifted off to sleep.

The Ant and the Grasshopper

Adapted by Catherine McCafferty
Illustrated by Jason Wolff

Summer had just begun. Animals and insects scurried about, enjoying the summer sun. "Summer's here! The best time of the year!" the Grasshopper sang. His joyful jumps took him from the cool shade of a bush into bright rays of the sun. "Warm sun, lots of fun!" he added to his song.

A line of ants marched past the Grasshopper, carrying small seeds and bits of food. As they walked along, some crumbs fell to the ground. Before the ants could get them, the Grasshopper had eaten the crumbs.

The biggest ant, at the end of the line, walked up to the Grasshopper. "We've worked very hard to gather this food," said the Ant. "You should have helped us pick up what we dropped."

"That's what's wrong with your summer song," the Grasshopper sang. Then he said, "You're always working. Summertime is for play, not work."

"Summertime is for planning and gathering," said the Ant. "It's time for getting all the food we will need for the winter."

"Winter is so far away, I think I'd rather go and play," said the Grasshopper. He was about to hop away when the Ant stopped him.

"Wait, my friend. What about all the food you took from us?" the ant asked politely.

"Oh, yes. Thank you." The Grasshopper pointed toward a field. "And over there is a whole field of wheat to replace your crumbs. I like cornfields better myself, but that might be too far for you to walk." And the Grasshopper hopped off to the cornfield.

The Grasshopper leaped onto a cornstalk. A soft leaf gave him a bed. Above him, another leaf gave him shade. And within reach, smaller, tender leaves gave him food. There was even an ear of fresh corn nearby.

"Those ants can gather and work and store. I'll just snooze right here and snore." He fell fast asleep.

Meanwhile, the Ant lined the tunnels of his home with seeds and other foods. "When the snow is on the ground, we will be nice and warm in our nest. We will have plenty of food to eat and plenty of time to play," thought the Ant.

All that summer, the Grasshopper watched the ants. When he saw them going to a picnic for crumbs, he hopped along to eat his fill. While they carried food back to their nest, he slept in his cornstalk bed.

Then one day, the Grasshopper heard a loud noise. The farmer was coming to harvest the corn! The Grasshopper jumped off his leafy bed and ran into the grass. Down came the leaves and the corn the Grasshopper had feasted on all summer. Down came the leaves that had sheltered him.

"Close call, all in all," sang the Grasshopper. "Did you see that?" he asked the Ant as the line of ants marched past. "I just lost my cozy bed and all my precious food!"

The Ant stopped. "The days are getting shorter, my friend. But there is still time for you to store food and find a winter shelter."

The Grasshopper thought about that for a second. "Not today, I've got to play," he sang and hopped his way through the grass. When he found a toadstool, he said, "This will put a roof over my head. So I'll just eat later . . . instead," he added, to make a rhyme.

The Grasshopper had just fallen asleep when he heard a plop! The next thing he knew, his toadstool was falling over.

"Oh, I'm sorry," chattered a squirrel above him. "My paws were so full of nuts that I dropped some. You can have them if you like."

The Grasshopper hopped away. "I don't like nuts, no ifs, ands, or buts."

All throughout the fields and forests, he saw squirrels gathering nuts. They chattered to one another, "I found more!" "Have you heard? This winter is going to be very snowy!" and "I think I have enough, but I want to be sure. It's going to be a long winter!" All this work was making it very hard to play, and to sleep. In a corner of the hay field, the Grasshopper found a small, sunny rock. He was just settling down, when the ants began marching by him again.

"You again!" he said to the Ant. "I thought by now you'd have enough. You can't eat all that stuff!"

The Ant smiled, but he was too busy to stop and talk with the Grasshopper. "My friend, it's always better to have a little extra than not enough," he called over his shoulder.

The Grasshopper frowned. The sun had moved, and the rock was cold. At the other end of the field, the farmer was cutting hay. "Doesn't anybody here know when to play?" he asked.

He hopped off to the apple orchard. Most of the leaves were gone from the tree. But the Grasshopper found a few small apples on the ground. He munched on them until he was full. Then he settled in for a nap near the root of the tree. The Grasshopper shivered. He looked around for a sunny spot, but the sun was already gone from the sky. "Someone needs to tell the sun that its working day is not done," he sang unhappily.

The sun was one thing the Grasshopper didn't mind seeing hard at work. But with each passing day, the sun that warmed him all summer long, seemed to be working less and less.

The ground seemed colder, too. One day, when the Grasshopper tried to nibble an apple, he found that it was frozen. "I don't like my apple in ice," said the Grasshopper. He was so chilly that it was hard to think of a second line to his rhyme. "Ice, nice, rice, mice . . ."

The Grasshopper tried to think of something nice. "A warm place with lots of rice," he sang in a shivery voice. He didn't especially like rice, but he was getting hungry. Then he thought, "Maybe I'll visit my friends, the mice." The Grasshopper crept into the home of the field mouse family. It was warm inside. There was no sign of rice, but the Grasshopper was sure they would have something else nice.

"Thank you for visiting, Mr. Grasshopper," said Mother Mouse. "I would invite you to stay, but all of my sisters and brothers are moving in for the winter. Isn't that nice? Oh, here they are now!"

A crowd of mice rushed into the nest. It was nice to see them hugging each other. But the Grasshopper wanted the kind of nice that meant he had a place to live and something to eat. The Grasshopper hopped back to the orchard. The ground was so cold that it hurt his tiny feet.

"Where are those ants, now that I need them?" sang the Grasshopper.

Suddenly snow began to fall. It covered the Grasshopper. With a jump, he fluttered his wings.

He had to get inside or he would freeze! Hopping as fast as he could, the Grasshopper raced to the Ant's home. "Anybody home?" he called as he stepped into the tunnels.

"Why aren't you out playing in the snow?" asked the wise Ant.

The Grasshopper wanted to say that he had just come by for a visit. But he could feel the cold wind on his back. Sadly, the Grasshopper sang, "I should have listened to what you said. Now I'm cold and scared and unfed." It wasn't his best song, but he hoped the Ant would understand and maybe help him.

The Ant did understand. But he wanted to be sure that the Grasshopper understood, too. "We got our food for the winter by working hard. If you stay with us this winter, you'll have to work hard, too."

The Grasshopper gulped. What if it was a long winter, like the one squirrel said? But then he remembered the ice and snow.

"Your job here will be to sing for us. Every day." Then the Ant laughed. "Because winter is our time to play."

All that winter, the Grasshopper sang for the Ant and his family. And the next summer, the Grasshopper sang a song as he helped to gather food. "Summer work is slow and steady. But when winter comes, I'll be ready!"

Brer Rabbit Outfoxes Brer Fox

Adapted by Megan Musgrave
Illustrated by Rusty Fletcher

I am going to tell you a story about Brer Rabbit and Brer Fox. But first, you ought to know a thing or two about rabbits and foxes.

Rabbits and foxes just never seem to get along. This is probably because foxes are always trying to make a meal out of rabbits, and rabbits are always trying to outfox those foxes.

Brer Rabbit was the craftiest rabbit ever to cross a fox's path. Brer Fox was always trying to catch Brer Rabbit, but Brer Rabbit always had a trick up his sleeve. One afternoon, Brer Fox decided to get Brer Rabbit once and for all.

"I'm a-gonna catch that hoppity rabbit and make me a fine meal outta him!" thought Brer Fox.

Brer Fox knew that Brer Rabbit liked to go over to the farmer's garden every day for carrots and cabbages. Brer Fox decided to hide behind a big tree on the road to the garden and wait for Brer Rabbit to pass. The tree was on the edge of a briar patch, full of bushes with thorns and burrs.

"I'm a-gonna wait right here for that sneaky rabbit an' cook 'im up in a rabbit stew!" said Brer Fox. He was very proud of his sneaky plan.

Soon Brer Rabbit came hippity-hopping down the road to the garden. Brer Fox jumped out from behind the tree and grabbed him up as quick as he could.

"I'm a-gonna brew a stew out of you, Rabbit!" said Brer Fox.

Brer Rabbit had to do some fast talking. "You can cook me up in a big ol' pot an' serve me for dinner, but please don't throw me into dat briar patch yonder!" cried Brer Rabbit.

Brer Fox thought for a moment. "Now, maybe dat stew would be too much bother for me. I'm a-gonna roast you up instead!" he said.

"You can fire up your ol' stove an roast me an' serve me up with fried taters, but please don't throw me in dat briar patch!" pleaded Brer Rabbit.

This was starting to sound like a lot of work to Brer Fox. He really just wanted to get that rabbit out of his hair once and for all. "Naw, your scrawny hide ain't worth troublin' over. I'm jus' gonna string you up from that ol' hick'ry tree an' git you outta my hair," said Brer Fox.

"You kin string me up an' jus' let me swing, but whatever you do, Mister Fox, pleeeaase don't throw me into that terr'ble briar patch!" cried Brer Rabbit.

Suddenly, Brer Fox knew just the thing to do. "Seems to me jus' about the worst thing I kin do is throw you into dat ol' briar patch, Rabbit," chuckled Brer Fox. "An' dat's jus' what I'm a-gonna do!" And with that, Brer Fox swung Brer Rabbit over his head and threw him into the middle of the briar patch.

"Yow! Oh, I'm a-gonna die!" yowled Brer Rabbit as he sailed through the air. But as soon as he landed in the briar patch, all Brer Fox could hear was Brer Rabbit hee-hawing and guffawing in gigglement. Brer Fox knew he'd been had again.

"Oh, Mister Fox, you shoulda known better! Y'see, I was born in dis here briar patch! I'm as happy as a crawfish in a river bed, an' now you're gonna have to find somebody else for dat dinner!" With that, Brer Rabbit bounced and bounded away through the briar patch.

Brer Fox was hoppin' mad. "I got to git dat rabbit good, once an' for all. He's a-goin' to Miss Goose's birthday party tomorrow, so I'm a-gonna make real friendly-like, an' go an' walk over to dat party with him. An' jus' when we git to crossin' over the river, I'm a-gonna throw dat rabbit in! He'll be gone for good, sure as shootin'!"

The next day, Brer Rabbit was at his house getting all spruced up for Miss Goose's party. When he saw Brer Fox come a-trottin' up his path he wrapped himself up in a blanket and acted real sick-like.

"What's all this moanin' and a-groanin' about, Rabbit?" asked Brer Fox.

"Oh, I'm sick as an ol' dawg, Mister Fox. I ain't a-gonna make it to Miss Goose's party after all," sighed Brer Rabbit.

"This is a-gonna help wit' my plan jus' fine," thought Brer Fox.

He said to Brer Rabbit, "Now, you know you gonna be sorry if you miss dat party, Rabbit. You come on wit' me, an' I'm a-gonna carry you."

"You're mighty kind, Mister Fox. But surely I couldn't ride on your back without a saddle," said Brer Rabbit sneakily. Brer Fox went off to find a saddle. While he was gone, Brer Rabbit picked a bunch of flowers for Miss Goose and hid them under his blanket.

Brer Fox came back wearing a saddle. "Up you go," said Brer Fox.

"You're mighty kind, Mister Fox, but surely I couldn't ride along in dis saddle without havin' a bridle to steer you along," said Brer Rabbit.

While Brer Fox went to fetch a bridle, Brer Rabbit rummaged around in his closet until he found a brown paper bag.

"I'm a-gonna give that fox a surprise he'll never forgit," Brer Rabbit said with a chuckle. "He thinks he can outfox me, but I'm the foxiest rabbit this side of the Mississippi."

When Brer Fox returned, he was wearing a bridle as well as the saddle. He was all ready to go just like an old horse at the starting gate.

"Rabbit," he said, "Miss Goose ain't a-gonna take it kindly if we're late for her party. You climb on up here now, an' let's git a-goin'." He chuckled to himself, thinking that soon he would be rid of that rabbit forever.

"Thank you, Mister Fox. You're terrible kind to an ol' sick rabbit like me," said Brer Rabbit with a groan as he climbed into the saddle.

As he was walking along, Brer Fox felt Brer Rabbit bustling around in the saddle. "What are you doin' back there, Rabbit?" he asked grumpily. He didn't like being Brer Rabbit's ride at all, but he figured this was the best way to get that rascal to the river.

"Oh, I'm fixin' up my blanket. I got a chill somethin' terrible, you know," moaned Brer Rabbit. But really he was pulling out that brown paper bag.

After another minute, Brer Fox felt his rider shifting and shuffling around again. "What are you up to now, Rabbit?"

"Oh Mister Fox, I'm just a-fixin' this ice bag on my poor ol' achin' head," groaned Brer Rabbit. But actually he was filling that brown paper bag with hot air.

Soon they came to the river. As Brer Fox stepped onto the wooden bridge that crossed over the water he thought, "I'm a-gonna throw that rabbit off into kingdom come. Yep, this is just the spot."

But Brer Rabbit was ready for Brer Fox's sneaky trick. As soon as he felt Brer Fox stop over the middle of the river, he pulled his feet out from under the blanket. "What you stoppin' for, Mister Fox?"

Brer Fox knew Brer Rabbit was up to something. He knew it was time to act. Brer Fox announced, "I'm a-gonna throw you into kingdom come once and for all, Rabbit!"

"Oh, no you're not, Mister Fox. Giddyup!" shouted Brer Rabbit. And with that, he threw off his blanket and popped that bag right over Brer Fox's ears.

BANG!

"Yeeoow!" shrieked Brer Fox. He thought a hunter had taken a clean shot at him. He jumped up in the air like a mad grasshopper and took off down the other side of the bridge.

Brer Fox galloped down the road toward Miss Goose's house with Brer Rabbit hanging on to the saddle and yodeling all the way.

"Giddyup, you ol' nag!" cried Brer Rabbit. Poor Brer Fox just kept on galloping along past the briar patch, past the farmer's garden, past the duck pond, and right up to Miss Goose's house. Miss Goose, Miss Sheep, and Miss Pig had heard Brer Rabbit yodeling from a long way off. When Brer Fox came galloping up with Brer Rabbit on his back, they thought they had never seen anything so funny.

"Brer Rabbit sure got Brer Fox's goat, all right!" clucked Miss Goose.

"Ol' Brer Fox won't want to go messin' with that rabbit agin, for sure!" bleated Miss Sheep.

"That Brer Rabbit is the trickiest critter this side of the Mississippi!" squealed Miss Pig.

"Whoa!" shouted Brer Rabbit as Brer Fox galloped up to Miss Goose's house. Brer Fox skidded to a stop and flopped on the ground right on the doorstep. "Aft'noon, ladies," said Brer Rabbit as he climbed down. "I am very sorry for bein' late, but my ol' horse here jus' don't run like he used to." Miss Goose, Miss Sheep, and Miss Pig nearly burst with laughter after seeing Brer Rabbit riding Brer Fox like a horse.

Poor old Brer Fox sat in the front yard, sputtering and gluttering and catching his breath. He was so mad he could spit. "That rabbit tricked me good dis time. I don' know how I'm a-gonna do it, but I'm a-gonna git dat rabbit one day, once an' for all," he fumed. Brer Fox felt a little bit better after tasting Miss Goose's birthday cake.

Ever since that day, sly ol' Brer Fox has kept trying to outsmart Brer Rabbit. And ever since that day sneaky Brer Rabbit has been just one step ahead of Brer Fox. So if you ever see a rabbit hopping around in a briar patch, or if you glimpse a fox snooping around a farmer's garden, it just might be ol' Brer Rabbit and Brer Fox trying to outfox each other again.

Androcles and the Lion

Adapted by Sarah Toast
Illustrated by Yuri Salzman

In ancient Rome there lived a poor slave named Androcles. His cruel master made him work from daybreak until long past nightfall. Androcles had very little time to rest and very little to eat. One day, he decided to run away from his harsh master, even though he would be breaking the law.

In the dark of night, Androcles got up from the miserable heap of straw and rags that served as his bed. Crouching low so he was no taller than the bushes that dotted the fields, the young slave moved swiftly away from his master's land.

Clouds covered the moon that night, and Androcles crossed the open fields unseen. It was only when he came to the wild woods that Androcles dared to stand up tall again.

Androcles found a sheltered place at the foot of a tall tree. There he lay himself down on a bed of pine needles and fell fast asleep.

When Androcles awoke, he hiked deeper into the woods so he wouldn't be found by his master. There he looked for water and something to eat. But other than a few berries, there was no food to be found anywhere in the woods.

Day after day, Androcles searched for food. And day after day, he went hungry. Androcles grew so weary and weak that at last he was afraid he wouldn't live through the night. He had just enough strength to creep up to the mouth of a cave that he had passed many times. Androcles crawled into the cave and fell into a deep sleep.

As Androcles lay sleeping, a lion was hunting in the woods nearby. The lion liked to sleep in the daytime and hunt for his food at night.

The lion caught a small animal for his supper. He ate his meal beside a stream in the woods. Then he set off for his cave as the morning began to fill the sky with light.

Just before reaching the cave where Androcles slept, the lion stepped on the fallen branch of a thorn tree. A large thorn went deep into his paw.

The lion let out an angry roar, which woke Androcles with a terrible start. From the mouth of the cave, Androcles could see the lion rolling on the ground in pain. The lion's roars echoed loudly in the cave.

Androcles was terrified that the lion would attack him. But the lion held out his hurt paw to Androcles. Even from a distance, Androcles could see the large thorn in the lion's paw.

Androcles found some courage and came closer. He slowly sat down on the ground near the beast. To Androcles' astonishment, the huge lion flopped his great paw into the young man's lap.

Androcles spoke soothing words to the lion as he carefully pulled the thorn from the lion's paw. "Don't worry, handsome lion. We'll have this thorn out in no time," he said softly. The lion seemed to understand that Androcles was trying to help him. When the thorn was gone, the lion rubbed his head against Androcles' shoulder and purred a rumbling purr.

Androcles was no longer afraid of the lion. The lion was grateful to Androcles and didn't even mind that Androcles had moved into his cave.

The lion slept most of the day. And at night, he hunted for food while Androcles slept. In the morning, the lion would bring fresh meat to Androcles, who would build a little fire to cook his meal.

Every morning after Androcles ate, he and the lion played for a while in the woods nearby. The lion showed Androcles how much he liked him by rubbing his head against the young man and licking his hands and feet. Androcles scratched the mighty lion behind the ears and petted his sleek and soft fur.

One morning, as Androcles was cooking what the lion had brought him, four soldiers suddenly appeared and surprised him.

"We saw the smoke from your fire," they said. "We have come to arrest you for running away from your master."

Androcles tried to run from the soldiers, but they were too fast for him. Two soldiers sprinted after Androcles. When they caught him, they tied his hands behind his back.

The lion awoke with a start. Before he could get to his feet, the other two soldiers threw a strong rope net over him. They attached two ends of the net to a stout pole and carried the angry lion out of the woods.

Androcles was forced to march to a huge arena in Rome. One soldier said to Androcles, "Your punishment is to fight a hungry lion!"

It was the custom in Rome at that time to entertain the people with battles fought on the sandy floor of the arena, which was circled by rows and rows of seats.

Suddenly, Androcles heard a trumpet blast. Then the bars to Androcles' prison were opened. A soldier pushed Androcles onto the field.

Androcles found himself alone in the middle of the huge arena. Hundreds of people were watching him, waiting for the battle to begin. When a lion's roar sounded, the people grew excited and a great cheer exploded throughout the arena.

The trumpet sounded a second time, and the bars to the lion's cage were opened. A lean lion bounded out of the cell, roaring with hunger. The crowd of people in the arena shouted, "Hooray!" The crowd sounded like another mighty roar in Androcles' ears.

The lion crouched only for a moment, but in that moment Androcles recognized his friend from the forest. The lion let out another thundery roar and bounded across the arena in three long leaps. He stopped right in front of Androcles—and then he gently lifted his big paw.

Androcles gave a mighty shout of joy. "Lion, you remember me!" he cried. He took the lion's paw in his hand and patted it lovingly. Then the lion gently rubbed his great head against the young man's shoulder. The two friends were reunited.

The crowd of people in the arena was stunned into silence. The Emperor motioned to Androcles.

"How did you tame this ferocious lion?" the Emperor asked Androcles.

"I merely helped him when he needed help, Your Highness," Androcles replied. "That is why he spared my life."

The Emperor freed Androcles and the lion. The lion returned to the wild woods, and Androcles became a free man in Rome.

Androcles often went for a walk in the woods to visit his good friend, who never forgot him.

Rikki-Tikki-Tavi

Adapted by Pegeen Hopkins
Illustrated by Richard Bernal

This is the tale of a brave mongoose, named Rikki-tikki-tavi, and his great fight to help a family that saved him. It all started and ended in the far-off land of India. It began on the first sunny day after many days of dark and rain. A young English boy named Teddy went outside to explore. There he found a mongoose in the road.

A mongoose is a small animal, a bit like a cat and a bit like a weasel. This mongoose, Rikki-tikki, had thick hair and a bushy tail that made him look like a cat. His skinny head and the way he moved his feet, though, were just like a weasel. Both his wiggly nose and his little eyes were pink. But when Rikki-tikki got mad, his eyes turned deep, deep red.

A big summer flood had washed Rikki-tikki out of the hole where he lived. The water carried him along and dumped him in a ditch just outside Teddy's house.

"Look, Mommy, a dead mongoose," Teddy said as he carried Rikki-tikki inside. "Let's have a funeral."

"No, Teddy," said his mother. "Maybe he's just wet. Why don't we dry him off?"

Teddy's father wrapped him in a towel to warm him up. The towel tickled Rikki-tikki's little pink nose. "Ah-choo!" The mongoose sneezed and then looked around. Rikki-tikki, like all mongooses, was a very crafty and curious creature.

Rikki-tikki ran up to Teddy and rubbed his wet head under the boy's chin. "Hey, that tickles," Teddy cried.

"He wants to be your friend," Teddy's father laughed.

"Wow, I can't believe it," said Teddy's mother. "He's a wild animal. I guess he's so tame because we've been kind to him."

"As long as we don't pick him up by the tail, or put him in a cage," said Teddy's father, "he'll run in and out of the house all day. You'll see."

Then Rikki-tikki scurried off. He spent the whole day running through Teddy's house.

First he went for a swim in the family's bathtub. Then he dirtied his nose, sniffing the ink in an inkwell. Later he burnt his nose while bumping it against Teddy's father's cigar. But at bedtime, he climbed up into bed right next to Teddy.

"Is that safe?" Teddy's mother asked. "What if Rikki-tikki bites or scratches Teddy?"

"He won't do that," Teddy's father replied. "Teddy is safer with him than if he had a guard dog watching over him. But if a snake were to come in here..."

Teddy's mother interrupted him. "Don't even say that," she said. They turned out the light. Teddy and Rikki-tikki went straight to sleep.

The next morning Rikki-tikki went out into the big garden at the back of the house to look around. It was a large yard with rosebushes as big as people. It had lime trees and orange trees, bunches of bamboo, and plenty of tall grass.

Rikki-tikki heard a sad song coming from the trees. He looked up and saw Darzee, the songbird, and his wife. One of their eggs had fallen out of their nest and a snake had come along and eaten it.

"Those snakes, Nag and Nagaina, are evil," Darzee cried. They weren't just any snakes. They were cobras, which are some of the biggest and deadliest snakes around.

"I'm sorry," said Rikki-tikki, "but I am new here. Who is Nag?"

Just then, a big black snake slithered up through the tall grass. It hissed a low breath that was cold and harsh like steam whistling out of a radiator. Rikki-tikki was so scared by the sound that he jumped back two feet.

The snake, five feet long from the tip of his tongue to the back of his tail, raised his head and its hooded back. He stared at Rikki-tikki with evil eyes that never blinked.

"Who is Nag? I am Nag. I am a cobra, and my family has been ruling this garden for thousands of years. Look at me and be afraid."

Rikki-tikki was scared for a second, but no more than that. He knew that as a mongoose, he was supposed to fight snakes. This was his duty. Nag knew it, too.

"Look out!" yelled Darzee's wife. At just that moment, another snake struck at Rikki-tikki from behind. He jumped high in the air as if he was bouncing on a trampoline. The snake, Nag's wife Nagaina, had tried to bite Rikki-tikki. She missed him by inches. Since a cobra bite can be deadly, Rikki-tikki was lucky.

Then, without a word, the two snakes quickly slithered off into the grass. Rikki-tikki went back to the house to see Teddy.

Later that night, Rikki-tikki listened to a peculiar sound. The house was silent, but Rikki-tikki could make out what seemed like the sound of snake skin rubbing on bricks. Nag or Nagaina was in the house! They had come in through the drain in the tub.

As quick as he could, Rikki-tikki ran off to Teddy's parent's bathroom. There he heard two voices whispering in the dark. It was Nag and Nagaina.

"When the house is empty of people," Nagaina was saying, "Rikki-tikki will have to go away. Then the garden will be all ours again. So long as the house is empty, we are the king and queen of the garden. Remember, our eggs in the melon patch will be hatching soon."

"Go in quickly," she said, "and scare off the people. Then you and I will take care of Rikki-tikki together."

Rikki-tikki's eyes glowed the deep red of a polished ruby. He watched as Nag's head came through the drain. He heard Nagaina slide away into the grass outside.

It seemed that Nag intended to wait in the drain until morning. Then the cobra could surprise Teddy's father when he got in the shower, scaring the man and his family away.

Rikki-tikki waited, too. He thought of all the nice things that Teddy's family had done for him. After an hour, he inched closer to the deadly snake. He would fight the snake and send him away for good. But he had to make sure that he bit the snake in just the right spot. One wrong move could cost Rikki-tikki his life.

Then without warning and as quick as a flash of lightning, Rikki-tikki jumped. He grabbed the snake by the back of the neck. Nag whipped his hooded head around. The snake swung Rikki-tikki like a limp rag doll. Still, Rikki-tikki held tight.

Then Rikki-tikki felt a burst of wind over his shoulder. He heard a large crack. Teddy's father had taken a large stick and hit Nag in the head. The black cobra lay still on the cold tile floor. Teddy's father quickly picked up the snake and got rid of him.

"Oh my," Teddy's mother cried from the bathroom doorway. "That mongoose has saved all our lives."

Rikki-tikki walked back into Teddy's room and spent the rest of the night there. When morning came, he knew he would have to find Nagaina and fight her, too. Once she found out that Nag was gone, she would be very angry. She would be very dangerous . . . to everyone.

Rikki-tikki went to the garden with a plan. "Darzee," he called to the songbird, "you have to help me. You must distract Nagaina while I go find her eggs."

Mrs. Darzee agreed to run over to where the black snake was lying in the grass and lure her away. Nagaina was sitting by the house and crying over her lost Nag.

"Oh no," exclaimed Mrs. Darzee so the snake could hear, "my wing has been broken and I can't fly." The bird, of course, was fine. She just needed to get the snake away from her eggs. Then Rikki-tikki could snatch them. As the bird fluttered down the garden path, Nagaina followed close behind, stalking her prey.

When he saw them pass by, Rikki-tikki ran over to the melon patch and began carrying off the eggs he found. He had just come back for the last egg, when Mrs. Darzee flew over to him.

"Oh Rikki-tikki, Nagaina has trapped Teddy and his parents on the porch of the house."

Rikki-tikki ran as fast as his legs could carry him. He reached the porch with the last of Nagaina's eggs in his mouth. Teddy's family had sat down to eat, but none of them moved. Their faces were as white as snow.

Nagaina stood inches away from Teddy's chair. She was ready to strike at any moment.

Rikki-tikki dropped the egg on the floorboard. He yelled, "Nagaina, I have the last of your precious eggs right here. I have taken all the others from the garden. This is your last one. Leave them alone, and I will give this last egg to you."

Nagaina spun around. She forgot everything for the sake of that one egg. As soon as she turned away from them, Teddy's father grabbed him and pulled him to safety.

Now Nagaina turned on Rikki-tikki, and a wicked fight began. The two animals moved round and round in an angry dance on the porch. But Rikki-tikki was very quick. He jumped back with each of Nagaina's wicked strikes.

From the stand-off, Rikki-tikki forgot about the egg for some time. After a few minutes, Nagaina got close to her treasure. Before Rikki-tikki could catch her, she snapped up the egg in her mouth and raced down the steps and out into the garden.

Rikki-tikki followed behind her, right on her tail. Over the garden paths they went: snake, egg, and mongoose. Perched above them was Mrs. Darzee, who watched the chase. She flew straight at the snake, hoping to slow Nagaina down a bit by cutting her off. She gave Rikki-tikki the chance to grab hold of Nagaina's tail. Rikki-tikki bit down just as Nagaina slid down into her hole.

Rikki-tikki went down into the hole with her. They continued the fight. The long grass at the entrance of the hole shook as the two struggled underground. Then the grass stopped waving. All the animals thought Rikki-tikki had lost.

Suddenly, Rikki-tikki's tiny head popped up out of the hole. "Nagaina has taken her egg and gone," he said. "She will never come back to this garden again."

Then he walked off to a sunny patch of grass and fell asleep. The tiny mongoose was content. He owed Teddy's family a big favor for saving him from the flood. By keeping his English friends safe from Nag and Nagaina, Rikki-tikki-tavi had returned the kindness.

THE
END